# FREAKING PURRFECT

*A Ridgeville Bite of Life Short Story*

## CELIA KYLE

# Freaking Purrfect: A Ridgeville Bite of Life Short Story

Maya has always wanted a hedgehog shifter in the Ridgeville pride. She almost stole one once, but she sorta went into labor before Operation Quill Catcher took off. Now, she wonders if having a werehedgie is all it's cracked up to be. After "borrowing" (kidnapping and/or saving... depending on who's asked) a werehedgehog her daughter has to run for her life, her mate has to take a life, and one of her sons thinks hedgehog is on the menu.

And as for the hedgehog... she's freaking purrfect.

*This short story is set in the RIDGEVILLE SERIES and does not stand alone. This is a little bite of family life for those who fell in love with the Ridgeville gang and aren't ready to let them go.*

# CHAPTER ONE

Ladies, if someone tells you that you'll forget the pain of childbirth, they're straight up liars. The reminder of that pain is a whining, crying, poop factory that sticks around until its eighteen, and its sole purpose in life is to clam jam its mother when she wants to get her freak on." -- Maya O'Connell, Prima of the Ridgeville pride and woman who most recently had her taco block-o-ed by the aforementioned spawns of Satan.

Maya hadn't killed her children yet, and she didn't want to ruin a nice fourteen-year streak over a...

Screw it. Yes, yes she did want to ruin the streak.

She breathed deeply and sought calm, trying very hard not to scream the house down. Her inner lioness told her to rip their den apart with her bare claws until they found the little rodents.

Not that her kids were rodents, but it was easier to kill them if she thought of them as mice and not, well, her kids.

*No, no, no...* She couldn't get rid of them yet. She'd have to wait until after dinner. If she hunted them right that second, she'd have to explain everything to Alex, and then *he'd* try to be the one to kill them. He was not stealing her bloody, claw-tipped thunder this time. Which meant she had to keep her overwhelming ragefire—anyone but her kids would get hatefire—under wraps.

She drew in another slow breath, fighting for a calm that seemed totally out of reach, and got a lungful of… *Alex.*

Alex, her mate.

Alex, the father of her children.

Alex, worshipper of the vagina. At the moment, she really wished he was in a worshipping mood because that was the only thing that would fix the hot mess surrounding her. And by hot mess, she meant the completely missing spread of bow-chicka-bow-bow-inducing delicacies that'd previously decorated the dining room table. All that was left were a few scraps and very familiar claw marks marring the solid wood surface.

If she had to tell her kids no claws in the house one more time… Well, she already planned on murdering them, so she'd just make sure it was painful.

Her mate's heat bathed her back, his thickly muscled arms sliding around her waist, and she leaned into him. She allowed him to take her weight while she tipped her head to the side, silently asking for what she craved. Fifteen years of mated life and she still couldn't get enough of him. Enough of his touch, his kisses, the feel of him sliding between her thighs…

Alex lapped at her mating mark, the scarring on her shoulder that announced she was one hundred percent taken. She shuddered and swallowed the whimper that leapt to her lips, pushing it back so they didn't draw attention. Having kids also meant being quiet during bow-chicka-bow-bow times.

But he knew. He always knew. He chuckled, warm breath

ghosting over her damp skin, and then clamped her flesh between his teeth. He bit down hard, not enough to break skin, but enough to make her body remember the night he'd first sunk his fangs into her. Her pussy clenched, memories of that night surging. That wasn't the only part of him that'd possessed her.

She let her eyes flutter closed, blinding her to the world that surrounded them, and she focused on her mate. Her lioness practically purred, the animal excited at having her mate so close. The beast wanted to rub all over him, coat them in his scent and then make sure he was coated in theirs.

Maya wiggled her ass, her pussy aching to be stretched by his cock. His rock hard cock. It nestled between her ass cheeks, his thick length prodding her rounded butt. Her center clenched, growing heavy and aching with a rising need. He could bend her over and…

Alex growled, his grip tightening, and small jolts of pain flared from her middle. His own lion wanted to come out and play, transitioning his human nails to a lion's claws. He could chase her through the forest and claim her once again. Fifteen years and she still wanted to be consumed by him at every opportunity.

The teeth clenching her shoulder lengthened and sharpened, his fangs growing to pointed tips that could easily sink through skin.

Maya pushed to her tiptoes, trying to force his hand to break through skin and renew her mating mark. Her clit twitched, anxious for Alex's attentions, while her nipples hardened and formed tight peaks. Her lioness purred and snarled, alternating between begging and demanding Alex get on with it already.

Chase her. Bend her over a stump. Claim her in front of the whole pride if he wanted to, but she… needed…

4

A bone-deep shudder raced through her, pushing her to the very edge of release, and she let loose a pleading whine. If he sucked a little harder... If he bit a little deeper... If he growled...

If he did, she'd come. Right then. Right there. In the middle of—

*"Guh-ross."*

Nothing killed happy sexytimes better than an eight-year-old.

Speaking of killing...

Maya straightened her spine and lifted her weight from Alex, all the while pretending she hadn't been two breaths from a wonderful Big-ish O.

The *Big* Big O actually came (*snerk*) during one of those fun chasey, claimy nights.

Her mate remained behind her, his whole body shaking while he buried his face in the hair at the back of her head. His cock remained a hard, solid presence and she once again hated the little snot nearby more than a tiny bit.

Maya pretended Alex wasn't silently laughing like a loon—he *always* thought being interrupted by the kids was hilarious—and focused on the small creature.

*Creature* being the operative word. What had happened to her little ball of adorable pink fluff of awesome?

"I grew up, *Mom.*" Said ex-adorable ball of pink fluff of awesome sighed. "And pink? *Gag.*"

Maya was pretty sure her daughter's first word had been gag. Not Mama or Dada. Or even theory of relativity like her BFF's kid, Cora.

Maya used to put cute little pink dresses on her daughter and then... *gag.*

At that moment, seven and a half years ago, her life had ended and hell began.

"What do you need, Harper?" Alex's muffled voice came from behind her, his deep tone vibrating through her still aroused body. Each syllable plucked her nerves, reminding her of what she'd been so close to mere moments before.

Before the hell spawn interrupted.

"The guests are arriving, and Aunt Carly said it's *rude* to stay inside and bump booties while everyone else is hungry." Harper jerked her tiny head in a small nod, those golden curls bouncing, before spinning on her heel and stomping toward the back door.

"Guests? Carly?" Those large, strong hands slid from her waist, up her sides and didn't stop until he cupped her shoulders. He encouraged her to turn and she moved with him. "Bump booties?"

Maya stared into those amber hued eyes. Eyes that would transition to a deep gold when he was close to losing control because he wanted her so much. Then they'd spark a bright yellow when angry.

She was pretty sure he was about to be angry, which totally couldn't happen because she was killing the kids first, dammit. They had ruined *her* plans—not his.

He hadn't bought the perfect steaks.

He hadn't hunted a great bottle of wine.

He hadn't bribed her guards to be *busy* for the evening. Well, longer distance busy-but-not-busy since they still needed protection. Just not all up on the front lawn protection. Maya made plans to make Alex roar, and the guys didn't need to hear all that.

Well, she'd *had* plans.

Plans her children apparently ate, which resulted in "Aunt Carly" but minus bumping booties.

"You have to promise not to kill anyone." She raised her

eyebrows and pointed at her mate, squinting her eyes slightly in a glare. She wanted his promise because she was going first, dammit.

"Maya?" He said her name but it had *that* tone. The one that said so much with so little and she glared harder.

"The thing about it is…"

"Maya." It was another of *those* tones. Dammit, he'd asked her a different round of questions that time.

"You know, *I* should be the angry one here." She wiggled out of his embrace, angling to blame everything on him and not her— or the kids. It'd let her keep her ragefire simmering without the risk of Alex stopping her. "Do you know what next week is?"

Alex frowned. "The Gaian Moon?"

"Yeah, but what else…"

The Gaian Moon came twice a year, a time when shifters were biologically driven to get hot and heavy with willing bodies. It was nature's way of ensuring shapeshifters thrived. It was also when she'd met Alex.

"Didn't you order a cow this year? Did you need me to organize pickup and delivery to Genesis?"

Genesis—their club and location of all things bow-chicka-bow-bow during the Gaian Moon. And if cow transport was all she needed, she had an entire pride of lions to order around.

"Cow…" She jerked back, staring at the man she loved more than life itself. "Organize…"

Did he really forget? Like, really, really? Okay, admittedly, life got in the way of a lot. They had three kids—two teenagers and an eight-year-old turning thirty tomorrow. Plus, they were the Prima and Prime of the Ridgeville pride. Between wrangling their lion shifter children and making sure the pride ran smoothly, they didn't have a ton of "us" time.

But he couldn't have... She took another step back. Had they grown so far apart that... God, could she finish a *sentence?*

Oh shit. The last time she couldn't finish sentences she was pregnant. Heaven help Alex if he knocked her up. She was too old and selfish to be a mother *again.* She was really enjoying being able to shove kids out of the door and it shut behind them without having to wonder if they'd be able to survive.

They knew how to shift, and they knew how to hunt. Her work was *done.*

Panic—*real* panic—took hold, wrapping around her throat and strangling her. Maybe the panic was a good thing. It'd kill her, and then she wouldn't have to worry about swollen ankles, big bellies, and stretch marks. That was good.

But if she died, she would really miss the Prince of Peen and his loyal subject, Duke Balls of Sack.

---

Alex wasn't sure if his mate was about to pass out from panic or anger. Even after fifteen years, it could go either way with Maya— which is what he loved about her. Life with her was never boring, and between her and their cubs, he was always kept on his toes. Hell, managing Genesis and controlling the pride were vacations from his time at home with those four.

As hectic as his days were, Maya made up for it every night. Every. Single. Passion-filled. Night.

And day if he could talk her into bending over the dining room table, or even just backing into the wall and wrapping her legs around his waist. His cock throbbed, arousal rising, and his lion grumbled and growled. It wanted to claim their mate. It wanted to dominate the female that belonged to them. He could already scent her arousal, her salty sweet cream preparing her pussy for him. Her nipples were hard, pebbled points straining against her bra and thin top.

He'd tear at her shirt and then tug one of those cups down, baring her breast. He'd take one nipple into his mouth and suck on the nub until she begged him to take her.

Alex's dick strained against his jeans, the tight fabric pinching his cock, and fuck he wanted her. His balls drew up tightly against him, anticipation thrumming in his veins. His gums ached, fangs pressing against his flesh while the cat fought for freedom. His nails pulsed with a stinging pain, the tips of his human fingers growing dark claws.

He shoved at the lion, kicking its ass back, but the beast remained in place and snarled at him. The animal could scent their mate's readiness and the desperate need to claim her rode him hard. Fuck her. Take her. Claim her.

His mouth watered, and he could practically taste her blood on his tongue. Sweet. Coppery. Perfect.

Maya continued to give him a wide-eyed stare—shock or panic? It didn't matter. He knew she craved him just as much as he ached for her. It'd take one pinch of a nipple, one flick of her clit, and they'd become lost to their passion.

Alex let his hands slide down her arms and over the fur peppered skin of her biceps before he shifted his touch to her waist. He didn't stop there, though. He wrapped his arms around her, hands meeting at her lower back before he reached down and cupped the abundant cheeks of her ass.

Fuck. So fucking soft and perfect, and he cursed himself for not putting a tube of lube in the dining room. The absence of lube didn't mean he couldn't play though.

"Alex," she whimpered, and he saw the change in her expression. If he didn't distract her, she'd start talking about other shit. Less talking. More sinking balls deep inside her.

He captured her lips with his own, sliding his tongue deep into her mouth and growling when her flavors slid over his taste buds. Maya shuddered and whined, her heat so close to his dick that he nearly came right there. More of her scent perfumed the air, sliding over his skin and covering him in her aroma. He wanted to taste her, to fuck her, to do every wicked thing he could imagine.

Twice.

Alex tightened his hold on her ass, bringing her flush with his cock, and he rocked his hips. His mate whimpered and did the same in return, the friction stroking his dick slow and hard.

Small hands slid over his shoulders, Maya clinging to him as she practically crawled up his body. Small pinpricks of pain told him that her own lioness wanted to come out and play as well. Those tiny nails dug into his skin so that the scent of his own blood crowded the air as well.

Fuck, he wasn't gonna be able to stop—not anytime soon—and those kids of his had better keep their asses outside if they wanted to live for another day. His kids and whoever the hell else showed up with "Aunt Carly" and her guests.

Alex backed Maya into the wall, his claw-tipped hands tugging and pulling on her skirt with each step. The second her back collided with the sheetrock, she lifted her legs. First one and then the other, and then she was fucking open for him—his dick. He tugged and yanked on the fabric, pulling it higher and higher until his fingers found bare skin—not even lace panties hiding her from him.

He wrenched his mouth from hers, the rough sounds of their

panting filling the air.

"Fuck, Maya." He caressed her ass, seeking her wet pussy. He first traced the crack of her ass, his mate wiggling and rolling her hips, silently begging him to toy with her dark hole.

"Is that what you want, baby?" he murmured low, his lion adding a rough rasp to his voice. He ghosted his fingers over her back entrance and that little pucker kissed the tip of one digit. "You want my fingers in your ass?"

Maya shuddered and wiggled even closer, crawling him like a fucking tree. Those nails scrambled for his flesh, seeking a hold so she could somehow take what she wanted. Not happening. He'd give pleasure—or not—at his own discretion.

"Tell me, Maya." He wanted the words because they got him just as hot as touching her.

Instead of asking for what she wanted, she pulled back and stared into his eyes—her she-cat glaring at him while she released a long, low hiss. Golden fur slid free of her pores, the lioness pushing forward even more, and he knew it wouldn't be long before the beast had Maya attempting to take what she wanted.

Attempting.

He let Maya have her way most of the time—was content to let her run wild and free—but he was still the Ridgeville Prime.

Alex released some of the control over his own cat, his eyes flickering and fur pushing past his skin. His flesh stung as each strand emerged, but it did nothing to lessen his fucking craving for Maya. His cock hardened further, nearly busting the zipper on his jeans, and he was tempted to let Maya get her way already.

Tempted, but not convinced.

He released one ass cheek and lifted his hand to fist her blonde curls, tugging her head back until their eyes met. "Tell me."

"Alex," she whined and wiggled, but he didn't move. He *wanted* to, but he wanted her begging first. Wanted her hot and wet and so needy she was nearly crying before he pounded her wet cunt.

"Say it." A garbled growl came from his mouth, the cat hovering at the edge of his humanity and just waiting for a chance to push forward and overtake his two-legged form. He didn't want to fuck in fur, dammit. He wanted skin on skin. Wet bodies and sweat slick limbs.

"Want..." Gold fur drifted up her neck. "Want..."

"For the love of... Neal, didn't I tell you they'd be in here fucking?" The soft padding of small feet over the old wood floors reached them. "They can't be left alone for a *second*."

Alex sighed and dropped his head forward, releasing Maya's hair as he laid his forehead on her shoulder. Maya groaned and did the same, hiding her face in his neck.

He wondered when rabbit could be put back on the menu. Sure, Carly—a rabbit shifter—was mated to Neal, one of Maya's lion guards, but Maya had plenty of other friends. Would she really miss *one*?

"I would, dammit," his mate grumbled. "But putting her in the hospital just long enough for us to fuck sounds good. All of them. All of them can go to the hospital. What can we do to take them out at once?"

He liked where his mate's head was.

"I heard that!" Movement to his left drew Alex's attention and he saw Carly's head poke around the corner. "And thank you for remaining clothed. Now, are you two done yet? It's been twenty minutes already."

Alex lifted his head and glared at the woman. Maya went one better and growled. Which did nothing for his rock hard dick.

"Do we smell done?" Maya sneered at her best friend.

Carly quirked a single brow. "I'm refusing to breathe. I've heard that old caves can suddenly accumulate deadly gasses and..." she shuddered. "You've popped out three kids and you're practically ancient. That's the Cave-Vag of Death right there."

Caves. Deadly gasses. Three kids. Vag of Death.

And that was all he needed for his cock to go from ready to pound nails to soft as an overcooked noodle.

"Bitch, you better run because as soon as I'm done riding my mate like a pony, I'm gonna cut your ass."

Wait, never mind. His mate threatening violence got his dick hard again.

"Can we press pause on the pony rides and delusions of actually catching me first? Because your kid is missing."

They both sighed at the same time, but Maya spoke first. This wasn't the first time they'd wandered off and it wouldn't be the last. "Benjamin or Gerald?"

Alex couldn't even find the energy to yell at his mate for calling their sons Ben and Jerry. Not when they were probably the reason he wasn't balls deep in Maya. Teenagers sniffing after some girl's tail.

"Neither." Carly shifted her weight, a small movement that his cat caught and focused on. He parted his lips and scented the air, attempting to confirm his suspicions. The flavors of Carly's emotions scraped his tongue and he narrowed his eyes at the wererabbit. She was uncomfortable—worried even. Why? "The thing about it is..." Never words he wanted to hear from Maya or her friends. "Dazs said she saw something at the tree line, and I told her to stay in sight while I finished setup, but then Cora decided she wanted to go 'Crouching Bunny' on her half-brother and *then* Zoey joined in because crouching bunny, hidden fox seemed like a good idea. When I turned around, Dazs was gone."

A low chuckle came from the direction of the kitchen, Neal obviously finding the events funny. Carly looked over her shoulder and glared at her mate before focusing on them once more—that worried expression in place. Apparently he didn't have the energy to bitch at Carly for calling Harper *Dazs* after Haagen-Dazs ice cream. "And Neal can't find her scent anywhere. Nothing but a hint of human and..."

Alex stopped listening after the word *human*.

He met his mate's gaze, hating the worry that clouded her eyes. Yes, they'd managed to get rid of Freedom all those years ago—the anti-establishment shifter group that'd kidnapped and killed so many of their kids. But that hadn't cleansed the world of all shifter-hating groups. Groups who would love to get their hands on the daughter of one of the United States' strongest—if not *the* strongest—Prime.

Maya's legs dropped from his waist and he held her steady while she found her feet. "Alex..."

"We'll find her."

And then he'd kill whoever took her. Or ground her for worrying her mother.

Maybe both.

He'd take away her TV and cellphone, too. The last time he'd outlawed texting, he'd been dubbed the evilest barbaric father in the world, but he'd take her hating him and still breathing than her love and no longer in his life.

# CHAPTER TWO

Kids, gotta love 'em even when they do stupid things and scare the shit out of you. Mainly because it's cheaper to let them live than hire a lawyer to mount a case for justifiable homicide." -- Maya O'Connell, Prima of the Ridgeville pride and woman who has that lawyer on speed-dial.

Maya wasn't going to let a little fear keep her down, at least not for long. She hadn't buckled when her best friend had been taken by Freedom, had she? Nope. She'd fucking fought. She'd held this pride together—okay, Alex had—and she'd do the same now. Okay, Alex would.

Then, when they found Harper, she'd either kill whoever laid their hands on Harper or she'd murder her own child.

Part of her hoped this was just another one of Harper's random wanderings in the forest. The ones where she did all she could to escape her own set of guards. Which was a hella-fun game when Maya was in on it and they formed a coordinated Strike Team of Doom.

When Maya and Alex weren't playing the same game? Not so much.

The second Alex gave her enough room to move, she took off, not bothering to see if her mate followed. He would—she had no doubt. He'd follow for now and then stand by her side when they found Harper. And *then* when they found her…

Maya would alternate between yelling and hugging her child while Alex handled the bloody killing parts when she was done yelling and hugging.

Maya's lioness grumbled and growled, annoyed that Alex would get to enjoy the kill, but it recognized his superior physical strength and lack of debilitating guilt. Not that she'd say the words aloud. Ever. The Holder of the Platinum Plated Hoo-Haa was a badass, after all.

They burst onto the back porch, and the gathered lions—some shifted, some not—scattered. They moved out of her and Alex's path, the more submissive of their pride dropping to their bellies with a whine while the stronger men and women slowly eased forward. She knew they just wanted to help. They might not know what had her and Alex on edge, but she was sure they could scent her panic and feel her mate's rage stretch across the land.

Her Harper… In the forest… A human scent so close to their den? That was never, ever a good thing, and the fact sent Maya's panic spiraling higher.

Their second, Grayson, strode through the crowd, her guards—Brute, Deuce, Harding, and Wyatt—right behind him while Ricker came from the direction of the forest.

They were all strong, determined cats who were loyal to the pride and to her and Alex. They would do whatever needed to be done to find Harper.

But they weren't Maya. They weren't Harper's mother. They didn't have the overwhelming biological need to destroy anything that stood between her and Harper.

Two familiar scents teased her nose—flavors that were a mixture of her and Alex plus something else only those two shared.

"Something's off."

"What happened?"

Two adolescent males spoke with the same voice. At least, everyone else thought they were the same, but Maya could tell the difference between them.

Maya answered, her gaze shifting to the tree line. It was smart to wait for Alex and the males to form a plan to search for Harper. But what was that saying? *Smart has the brains, stupid has the balls.* Well, she had a set of brass ovaries and her sons... she didn't want to ever think of her teenage sons' balls. Ever ever.

She hated to say the words aloud, but they had to be said. "Harper's missing. Ricker scented a human."

The first growl came from Easton, but she was more worried by Weston's reaction. He'd always been her silent killer. The one who'd remain quiet until he snapped the head off a chicken in one bite. Very gross thing to watch a two-year-old do, by the way.

She reached out, not stopping her slow sweep of the trees with her gaze, and wrapped her fingers around West's wrist—his thick, furred wrist. His hand was already half shifted, his inner lion nearly free of her son's control. Not a good thing.

"We'll find her, West," she whispered and then reached for Easton on her left. She rubbed his back, stroking away the unending growl. "We'll all find her."

"Mom." The single word was hardly more than a snarl, West losing the battle to his cat. "Humans. Council. Ricker."

17

Yeah, the first two were definite threats to them—the shifter council mostly because it'd become a corrupt institution that she and Alex often told to fuck off. They were happy in their small corner of the world, and if they tried to impose laws on Ridgeville… Well, Alex and Maya were quickly disabused of the notion. Was Harper's disappearance related to Maya's most recent "suck my dick" message?

As for Ricker… He was a council trained tracker who'd joined the pride nearly fifteen years ago and a tiger unquestionably loyal to Ridgeville.

"It's probably nothing. She's just playing a trick." *Please let it be a trick.* "Ricker will find her."

She wished she could believe her own words.

Easton leaned close, his voice low, as if whispering would keep everyone else from hearing. "Brody said he saw a strange tiger last night."

Maya whipped her head around to meet her son's stare. "And he didn't say anything to his father? To me or Alex?"

Brody was a good kid, younger than Maya's twins and Ricker's oldest son, a tiger shifter determined to run in his father's footsteps. But he should have said something. They didn't rule Ridgeville with an iron paw, but they sure as fuck knew who went in and out of their town.

"It could be nothing." Easton said the right words, but he didn't sound as if he believed himself.

"What else did Brody say? Where is he?" Maya wrenched her focus from the forest and scanned the gathered crowd. Her gaze touched on kids that were practically her own—Zoey, Cora, and Katie silently huddled on the back porch steps. Elijah, Carson, and Ryan—Neal's sons from other Gaian Moons—standing guard nearby. Brute's son Kier balanced on the railing, his stare missing nothing as he scanned the yard as well. He was easily just as large as his father—perhaps even bigger—but lightning fast and silent like his fox mother.

Fingers still wrapped around West's wrist, she knew the exact moment he spied something. His heart rate picked up, the pulse beneath her fingertips racing while his body twitched, as if it just waited for permission to run and pounce on whatever had caught his attention. She snapped her head around and followed her son's line of sight, hunting for whatever had him primed and ready to go.

She didn't understand at first, couldn't wrap her head around the flashes of gold that burst into sight for a split-second only to disappear. Another flash of burnished amber. Then... that small spark of gold broke through the bushes.

Small. Familiar. *Hers.*

A tirade leapt to Maya's lips, the words hovering on her tongue and waiting to be released as soon as Harper drew near enough. Except, the blur ran as if the devil chased her. Those small paws and smaller claws dug into dirt and grass, clumps flying through the air in her wake. She raced toward the house, ears pressed flush with her skull, fur nearly flat against her body with the rapid speed.

The mad dash wasn't what had her—and her two sons—on edge. It was Harper's eyes—the whites clearly visible and the stark terror on her lioness-shaped face unmistakable. Her daughter ran for her life—as if death nipped at her heels and threatened to swallow her whole. Something chased Harper from the forest, from whatever mischief she'd tumbled into, and it was enough to send her blindly running back home. The fur on her sides was damp and darkening, slick with sweat even though natural lions didn't, and her chest heaved with every rapid lope. Exhaustion pulled at her baby, but Harper kept pushing and pushing.

What had her running—

What had her running suddenly burst into sight as well.

Black. White. Orange. Her human mind immediately registered "tiger" but her lioness saw even more. It saw bloodthirst. It saw death. It saw carnage.

The tiger chasing Harper wouldn't stop until she was dead.

Unfortunately, he hadn't yet realized he was a dead tiger walking.

At the moment, it was a matter of discovering who'd get to the male first—Maya with her rapid shift and quick reflexes or Alex with his longer stride and (slightly, but really greatly) superior strength.

---

Alex's lion had him moving before his human mind acknowledged the sight before him. His transition rolled through him like a raging wave, the tsunami of his shift snapping bones and stretching muscles faster than he could register. He took one step and then another, his clothes ripping at the seams while his cat's body emerged. Hands and feet became paws, his teeth lengthened to become fangs, and his mouth reshaped to form a deadly maw. He was a running, roaring, four-hundred pounds of muscle and pain.

Pain he would give to the intruder.

Harper sprinted across the flat land, panic-stricken eyes locked onto him, and he could practically hear her cries for help. Fear made her run harder, race faster, toward safety. To him.

And he wouldn't disappoint her. He wasn't just her father. He was her *Prime*—the one lion above all others who protected the pride.

He dug his claws into dirt and grass, long nails tearing at the earth beneath his paws. He raced across the wide expanse, his attention split between his daughter and the tiger on her tail.

The soon to be dead tiger. He could have tolerated an intrusion—Brody had come forward and admitted what he saw—but the trespasser had to go and do something unforgiveable.

He scared Alex's little girl.

His little girl now soaked in sweat, eyes filled with tears, and a stare that pleaded for help.

The second he got close enough, he leapt over Harper and landed with a low thump in front of the tiger, a thump and a roar so loud the ground shook. He hissed and bared his fangs, showing the male exactly what he'd get if he pushed. The tiger skidded to a stop, his claws sinking into the ground as he slipped over the dried grasses until he finally came to a stop less than ten feet from Alex.

It was ten feet too close as far as he was concerned. Way too close to him, to his family and to his pride.

The tiger hissed in response, fangs dripping with saliva, the craving for blood still filling every inch of the cat's body. His striped tail flicked, the tip twitching with agitation, and his opponent rose to his full height. He padded back and forth in front of Alex, those eyes trained on the pride at his back and not the lion so close to him.

Stupid, that.

Alex hissed at the male and pulled his lips back, baring his fangs while he went into motion as well. He mirrored the intruder's path, keeping pace while the male sought a way around him.

The only way to get to Harper was *through*, not around. Through Alex, and if his opponent managed to take him down—doubtful—he had to get past Grayson, the guards, and Maya and their sons.

He'd put his money on Maya and the twins.

Except the tiger was an idiot, or too stupid to care about the danger he'd put himself in. He bunched his legs beneath him, massive muscles tensing, and Alex prepared himself. It was a lazy cat that had to prepare for an attack so blatantly. The male hadn't trained for combat—hadn't had his life and the lives of his loved ones dependent on his ability to kill.

Alex had. Through his fights with Freedom and altercations with HSE—the Humans for Shifter Extermination—he'd had plenty of practice.

The tiger finally got the opportunity he'd been waiting for, and Alex bolted into action. His opponent went high, trying to leap over Alex, but Alex went higher. He rose to his back legs, forelegs stretched and claws flexed, and dug the sharp nails into layers of fur, skin, and flesh. He curled his nails around whatever muscle and fat he found, pulling at the body above him as it continued its arched path. He yanked and fell forward, claws digging through the male from chest to hips in a single, rending pull.

The coppery tang of blood filled the air, the putrid stench of his opponent's aroma nearly making him gag with the smell. But he didn't have time to get sick. He had to keep the pressure on the male while he had an advantage. So he spun in place and brought his foreleg around, striking out at the male once again. Claws met flesh and then bone, nails finding home in the male's hip.

He yanked down, traced the line of the male's back leg, and opened him up from hip to ankle. The male would be bled dry by the time Alex was done.

The tiger stumbled back, fur stained red from his wounds, flesh and fur dangling from his body, but determination still filled his expression. Alex's opponent wasn't giving up. Not yet.

Which meant the only way things would end was with death.

The tiger darted forward, jaws snapping, teeth coming within inches of Alex's head, but he didn't give a damn. His training had him staying out of harm's way without thought. The cat moved on instinct, avoiding each deadly swipe while he subconsciously delivered his own brand of pain and death.

He twisted and turned, ducking low and aiming high while his claws remained unsheathed. The scent of the male's blood soaked the air, blinding him to any others, and its presence drove his cat's bloodlust to rise even higher. It wanted to bathe in the red liquid, soak the earth, and watch as life left his opponent's eyes.

*Yes*, he mentally hissed. That sounded like an excellent plan.

The tiger darted forward once more, snapping his long, white fangs, and Alex easily danced out of reach. He took that moment to deliver another round of pain, nails scraping fur and flesh until he struck bone.

More blood flowed freely until the dirt was stained red with the sticky liquid. So much coated the grass that they no longer fought on dry ground but in mud.

Thankfully none of the blood was his own.

A long slow hiss sounded behind him, the feline threat followed by a low grunt he recognized. He mentally smiled. The grunt came from Brute, the hiss from Maya. The guard obviously doing his best to keep Maya restrained, and his mate wasn't taking it easy on Brute. He had no doubt that she'd gladly join the fight and rip out the male's throat. He had strength, but Maya had agility, cunning, and bone-deep stubborn determination. Fuck, but he loved her. Her, the family they'd started, and the pride they'd built.

23

A red paw swung at his head and Alex jerked out of reach, glaring at the tiger. This male was a threat to all he held close in his heart, and it was time for him to die. He was done playing—done causing pain—and was now ready to put an end to the carnage.

So when his opponent rose up and stretched for Alex's head once more, Alex ducked low and spun. The tiger went over his head, the leap taking him to Alex's opposite side. To the casual observer, it'd appear as if the tiger succeeded in his attempt to get past the Prime, casual observers that hadn't been trained by Ricker or Stone—the strongest gorilla shifter he'd ever met. Strong and deadly and more than willing to kill for what he believed in.

Years ago, when they'd begun training shifters in the mountains of Ridgeville, he'd believed in making sure their people could protect themselves and others—training Alex used to rip out the tiger's throat.

One snatch, one grab of his claws, and he held a mass of flesh on his paw. The tiger fell to the ground with a hard thump, body twitching and paws scrambling to bat at his throat. With the pain and panic came the cat's retreat while the male's beast shoved his human half forward.

While the tiger struggled for breath, fur receded and claws transitioned, the animal reverting to its two-legged form in a rapid succession of snapping bones and stretching muscles. The jagged wounds came into view, flesh wrested from bone and dangling from his stomach and ribs. Pale splashes of white shone through the red, attesting to the depth of Alex's strikes. He'd wanted to visit pain on the male—pain and death.

And he'd succeeded.

Alex rested on his haunches and shook his paw, sending that hunk of flesh flying through the air to land near the tiger's—

male's—head. Panicked eyes met his, agony filling his opponent's features as pain and the truth finally registered.

He was a dead man.

Alex watched the shifter die on his lawn, his pride bearing witness to his rapid and deadly response to a threat.

Then he lifted his paw and ran his rough tongue over the thick padding, cleaning it of blood and gore.

Like all cats, he really hated to have anything on his paws.

# CHAPTER THREE

Be careful what you wish for. Also be careful to include a clean-up in your wish. Because when that shit comes true, sometimes it comes with a dead body, and I don't do cleaning. Ick." -- Maya O'Connell, Prima of the Ridgeville pride and so not into dealing with messy things.

Brute didn't release Maya until the human-shaped tiger was well and truly dead.

Dammit.

But the fight was over, her mate was well, and her daughter...

Harper remained plastered to the backs of Maya's legs. The small, damp fur-covered body trembled and pressed closer. The short snout and broad forehead nestled against the back of her knees, as if hiding her face from the carnage made her invisible.

And that... broke her heart. They were a family of lions, a pride that had stood strong against every enemy that'd come their way, but Harper was too young...

Too young to have to face reality, at least not yet. It broke her heart that she'd already been exposed in this way.

Harper shook again, the violent tremble so strong Maya nearly tumbled forward, and she reached out for Brute to steady her. The forearm beneath her palm was furred with the golden strands of their kind, and a glance around the yard revealed that *everyone* was in some stage of shifting or another.

Alex had been the first to react, but the rest of their pride looked just as ready to step in—like the solid, protective family they'd always been.

Harper rubbed her snotty nose on Maya's calf, a soft sniffle immediately following, and Maya didn't want her daughter to emerge and be faced with the gore.

She squeezed her guard's arm. "Brute?" The massive male turned his attention to her. "Can you and the other guys," she jerked her head toward the remnants of her mate's opponent, "take care of things while I see to…" she flicked her gaze to Harper and then back to him.

"Of course," he murmured and turned his focus to the crowd.

A raise of his hand and quick gesture had people moving, her personal guards stepping forward while others focused on gathering kids and ushering everyone inside. The pride worked as one—squirrel, tiger, fox, or rabbit—they got shit done.

Which meant Maya could focus on her mate and children. As others drifted away, Alex drew closer. He didn't stop until he reached her side and nudged her palm with his nose. She ran her fingers over his snout and then dug them into his mane, the fur not even a hint damp with sweat. He didn't breathe heavily from exertion, and she didn't even catch a hint of his blood in the air.

He was letting her see that he was okay.

He was okay. Their daughter was okay. Their sons were okay.

27

So that meant she could fall apart. But she wouldn't because badass Primas didn't fall apart when the very reason they breathed was threatened. She had brass ovaries, right?

Maya fisted Alex's fur and he leaned into her, giving her the strength she needed. His touch, his strength, allowed her to turn, take a tiny step back, and then fall to her knees in front of Harper.

The tiny lioness trembled, whiskers twitching, ears flat against her head and tail whipping back and forth. Her lips shook as well, a mixture of a lion's whine and a child's cry escaping her throat.

"Oh, baby," she whispered and held out her arms. "Come here."

But Harper didn't rush at her, not like she had in the past when she needed reassurance. When Alex turned fully to face their daughter and released a low chuff, she still didn't move. If Harper didn't want mommy, she *always* wanted daddy—and yet she remained in place.

No, she actually took a step back.

Easton lowered to a squat on Maya's other side, Weston just behind him on two legs with fur coating every inch of skin. "Harps?" He held out his hand, palm up as if he beckoned a frightened animal. "Come here. Dad took care of things, right? You're okay."

The trembles and shakes didn't cease, not when Harper's attention drifted from her brothers to her father and then landed on Maya once more. Broken eyes. Sad eyes. Eyes that'd seen too much at such a young age. She wondered what really haunted her little girl.

What...

Harper jerked, a full body shake, and then lurched forward. She rose to all fours, another jolt overtaking her, and Maya's eyes filled with tears. The third lurch had one droplet trailing down her cheek and then a fourth…

The fourth ended with a small maw spread wide, a high-pitched yowl that signaled her daughter's pain and… And a teeny, tiny hedgehog rolling from Harper's mouth.

Her daughter.

Tried to eat.

A hedgehog.

Maya stared at the small bundle, its curled body hardly moving, and then let her attention flick to Harper, then the dead tiger behind them, and once more to the hedgie. She just shook her head, unable to do much more than wonder and stare.

Weston could do more though. When Alex, Maya, and East froze in place, West snarled and then roared, jumping over his brother and aiming straight for the animal. A true beast or shifter?

"Weston, no!" She reached for her son, rushing to stop him from doing something he'd later regret. With his animal so close, so reckless and uncontrollable… He'd drown in the guilt when he was himself once more whether this was a natural animal or a tiny shifter.

Alex moved as well, his jaws parting to release a roar, muscles bunching to tackle their son.

But it wasn't them that stopped Weston in his tracks.

It was Harper. Harper who darted forward to stand over the hedgehog, protecting it—her?—with her body. She opened her mouth and released a long, slow hiss, short fangs exposed and pure fury in every line of her feline body. It was pure, momma-esque rage that Harper unleashed on her older, larger, stronger brother— a child's fury that had him backing away while his fur receded as quickly as it'd come.

They all stood there, their family of lions—every one of them on the edge of losing control, and Maya... She did what she always did. What she did best...

"Dazs, you are grounded, young lady." She adopted her mom tone and even wagged a finger at her daughter. "Mommy said she wanted a hedgehog in the pride, but we agreed we'd plan Operation Quill Catch together." Maya widened her eyes, mouth dropping open a little with feigned shock. "Oooh, just wait until your Aunt Carly gets ahold of you."

A second story window slammed open and Carly leaned out. "Did she seriously run Operation Quill Catch by herself? Dazs, you little shit! Just wait until I—"

Choruses of "little shit" came from inside the house, the all-too-familiar voices of children filling the air.

And that was enough to pop the tension-filled balloon that surrounded them. Alex gave himself a full body shake and relaxed, leaning into her side. Weston took a deep breath and cracked his neck, his fur fully receding with the new calm that washed over him. Easton pushed to his feet and stepped closer to a rapidly calming West. Shoulder to shoulder, they stood and took strength from each other. Which just left Harper and her little friend.

Her little trembling, saliva soaked, hedgehog-shaped friend.

What the fuck was she supposed to do with a *hedgehog*?

---

An hour later, alone with just the hedgehog and a still-shifted Harper, Maya got her answer. What was she supposed to do with a hedgehog?

Fill the sink with water and let it take a bath—a human-shaped Mommy and tiny lioness assisted bath.

Harper purred, hind legs on the toilet seat and forelegs on the counter, and occasionally lapped at the hedgehog as she floated past. Every so often Harper and the hedgie would freeze, gazes snapping to the bathroom door, their heads tilted as if they listened for an approaching predator.

Maya's heart broke for them. She wasn't sure of the hedgehog's age, but until that day, Harper hadn't had to worry about predators. Now it was all different. Her baby wasn't such a little baby anymore.

Maya cupped the small animal, cradling the nearly weightless body in her hands, and carefully lifted until they were eye level. "Hi, sweetheart. You had a rough day, huh?"

She stroked its small head, careful to keep the pressure light while she gathered its scent. She brought her fingertips to her nose and Maya's lioness was there, ready to identify the small bit of quill-covered animal in her palms. Yup, hedgehog shifter. A girl, though she wasn't sure of her age. Regardless, Harper brought her home. Harper was Maya's. That meant the hedgehog was Maya's.

Period.

"Do you want to shift for me?" She raised her eyebrows, her blue eyes locked on the near black of the hedgehog. "Maybe tell me what happened?"

The hedgie's response was immediate, tiny squeaks interlaced with snaps of her teeth and wiggling of her body. She fought to get free of Maya's grip, but she wasn't about to release the small shifter. Not at that height. Not when the fall could possibly kill her.

Unfortunately, Harper made the task even more difficult. Maya's daughter yowled loud and long, ending the cry with a drawn out hiss that promised violence. It would have scared Maya if she hadn't given birth to the kid. After shoving a wiggling watermelon—three wiggling watermelons—there was no pain that she couldn't tolerate and live through.

A bite from her kid was *nothing* compared to child birth.

No-thing.

That didn't mean her wonderful, accommodating, protective-as-hell pride felt the same way.

Brute broke the door down.

Carly dove between the male's legs and slid across the floor, not stopping until she struck the opposite wall. Maya would have laughed at her BFF since Carly was rocking a rabbit nose, two whiskers, and floppy ears, but somehow she restrained herself. She should congratulate the wererabbit. She'd been practicing a partial shift for years but still hadn't quite gotten the hang of it. She was doing better, right?

Maddy was next, the little Sensitive climbing up Brute's back and launching her shifted body over the larger male. Maddy—after her badass lessons all those years ago—had become more of a "rush in now, figure out what I'm doing later" lioness. Which was why she went scrambling across the tile as well. Lion claws plus slick tile didn't really work.

Elly rocked her squirrel super powers. Oh, she climbed Brute but then hopped to the top of the door, one hunk of wood still clinging to the hinge. Then it was another leap to a curtain followed by a balancing act along the top of the glass enclosed shower. The squirrel shifter didn't stop until she perched on the closest corner, beady little eyes narrowed and focused on the hedgehog in Maya's hands.

And Maya... she just sighed and shook her head. God love the pride, but they overreacted just a little. That feeling doubled when Brute stumbled into the bathroom, pushed by Millie's large, black, panther head right to the back of his legs. On her furred heels came the rest of her guards.

Behind *them*? Her mate. Alex—a sight for sore eyes and bleeding fingertips that were caused by one particular hedgehog, a hedgehog that went from attacking Maya to crawling up her bare arms and cowering in her hair.

She let her gaze touch on each member of her family. They were more than pride after the years they'd fought side by side. "Y'all are batshit crazy with a side of what the fuck are you doing?"

Harper chuffed her own little addition, her support clear.

Alex gave her a grin, a small tip of his lips that had her both hot and aching for a bed and annoyed at once. Damn the gorgeous hunk of lion. He made it even worse by leaning against the doorjamb—legs crossed at his ankles and arms over his chest. His thin shirt stretched taut over those hard muscles she loved so much and—

Carly grunted, the sound drawing Maya's attention, and then scrambled to her feet, tiny claws tipping her fingers clicking and clacking on the tile. "We're *rescuing* you."

"Uh-huh." Maya rolled her eyes. "Right. From a hedgehog."

"Shifter," Carly added, and the squirrel added her own animalistic *yeah*-chitter.

"Right. Hedgehog shifter." She pointed at her neck. "The teeny tiny hedgehog shifter currently cowering in my hair? That's the one you're worried about?"

Every single woman—shifted or not—focused on the small lump at the back of her neck.

Even Brute glared at the ball. "Close to your jugular. One bite and…"

And the hedgehog in question squeaked in outrage. Maya had

gotten good at shifter interpretation. This one basically said, "Well, I never."

Unless the hedgie was young. Then it was "nu-huh, poopie head."

Age had a lot to do with it all, and that was one thing Maya still didn't know.

Because the woman-girl-person wouldn't shift.

Maya turned her attention to her mate and did what any self-respecting woman would do—she whined. "Aleeexxxx…"

He just chuckled, that sexy one she loved so much. "All right, guys. She's safe. Get out."

"But—" Carly started.

Maddy hissed.

Elly flew at her like crouching squirrel but never actually landed because Harper launched herself at her Aunt Elly, which had Elly's mate Deuce getting all snarly and—

"E-fucking-nough!" Maya's own roar cut through it all. The shout echoed off the walls, filling the space with its volume, and everyone froze in place. Even Elly, captured in Harper's slobbery hold, stopped wiggling to get away.

All eyes were on her, human and animal alike, and she took advantage of the momentary quiet.

"That's enough." Maya pointed—once more—at the cowering hedgehog. "This little hedgie girl is scared shitless." At least, she hoped so. She really didn't want to get shit on. She thought she'd moved past that once the kids were potty trained. "You guys aren't making it better, so get your poop in a group and get the fuck out."

Males grunted their objections and Elly squeaked, although Maya wasn't sure if that was in outrage or pain because Harper hadn't let her go yet. Maddy chuffed, Elly curled her midnight lip and exposed a single fang, while Carly…

Well, another one of Carly's whiskers busted free.

Maya wasn't going to laugh. She wasn't. At least, not until they were all gone.

Which wasn't happening because everyone remained motionless. Dammit.

"I'm not joking. I want you all gone." She swung her attention to her daughter. "Harper, put Aunt Elly down before Uncle Deuce turns you into a Scooby Snack." She didn't stop there with giving orders. "Brute, go order me a new door. Carly, so help me, if you scratched my new cabinets with those chiclet nails of yours. And Maddy," Maya sighed. "Honey, bless your heart and thank you for coming to my rescue, but get the fuck out."

Those orders earned her two things—glares and an empty bathroom. Alex even managed to get Harper out of the space.

Which left Maya with a hedgehog. What the fuck was she supposed to do with a *hedgehog*, again?

# CHAPTER FOUR

Don't ever have kids. Mainly because when you see your mate being all sweet and it makes you want to ride him like a pony, they clam jam you *again*." --Maya O'Connell, Prima of the Ridgeville pride and woman who often has her muffin muzzled by the little bastards. Er, darlings.

Upstairs was quiet, most of the pride gone while his mate's guards and her "posse" headed back downstairs to the living room. Nah, "posse" wasn't the right word. What did she call their group? Then he snorted.

*The Ovulators.*

God save him from crazy women, though his life sure as hell would be boring without them.

The small lioness in his arms sniffled and rubbed her snout on his neck followed by a low purr. His baby girl's furred body was a warm weight balanced on his forearm, and he tightened his hold a little more. He'd nearly lost her. One stumbled step, one hitch in her stride, and that tiger would have been on Harper.

Alex's lion stirred, growling at the mere idea that they'd almost lost their cub. Harper was *theirs*.

Theirs and trembling and scared... The stench of her fear still burned his nose, still surrounded him and stoked the cat's need for vengeance—even though they'd already done their job.

Alex padded down the hall, passing his sons' rooms, both boys playing some mindless video game rather than thinking about Weston's near miss. He still hadn't figured out how the hell to help West. It was as if his control lessened with every day that passed, and he sure as hell didn't want to track his own son when he truly lost his grip on humanity.

Cuddling Harper close, he nudged open the door to her bedroom, the explosion of pinks and purples searing his eyes for a moment. He blinked to clear his vision, the hot pink ceiling making his eyes water.

Harper hated pink clothes but loved the girly colors in her space. It made his kid—and his mate—happy, so he dealt with it.

He didn't stop until he reached her tiny princess bed and carefully lowered himself to the soft surface. He repositioned his cat-shaped daughter, making sure she was braced on his thighs before he rubbed his cheek on the top of her head. He released a low, rumbling purr, telling the cat that all was safe. Harper was well and protected, and it could retreat now. His daughter simply whined and tried to get even closer, as if she could dig beneath his skin and being that close was her only safety.

Another purr with an added chuff. Encouragement from her Prime, not her father. Daddy kissed boo-boos. Primes—leader of the pride—kept the pride safe.

Just like he'd always keep Harper safe.

"Come on, sweetheart. Shift back for me." He'd force her if he had to, but he *really* didn't want to go that far. It'd make Harper's shift painful *and* it'd piss off Maya. "Daddy needs to know what happened, huh?"

Alex rubbed his cheek atop her head again, his purr still gently rolling from his throat while he waited Harper out. His kids were all different—their personalities as individual as Maya's favorite ice cream flavors. His Harper was slow to make choices. She weighed her decisions and carefully determined possible outcomes before taking action.

Which was what made her mad dash—and kidnapping of a hedgehog—so odd.

He remained in place, his hands gentle while he traced her spine, his purr soft while he nuzzled the top of her head. He wasn't sure how long they sat there, father and daughter coming to a silent agreement to figure out what the hell happened.

And eventually, Harper gave in. It began with a single snap of bone, a jarring crack that was immediately followed by another and then another. Fur receded and was quickly replaced by skin. Paws returned to hands and feet while the heavy muscles of her lioness shrank to his little girl's thin limbs. For all the cracks and breaks, the shift passed in a gentle roll, the transition smooth as silk and done within moments—which meant he now cradled a nude little girl. One that trembled and cried with huge tears escaping her eyes. But the tears didn't have him wondering if there really was someone who could conjure the dead. It was the bruising—the purple that marred Harper's forehead and the large swath of dark near black on her side.

"Sweetheart." Harper shook and he grabbed a nearby blanket—one they kept on hand for moments like this. "Why didn't you shift back sooner, huh?"

38

Alex kept his voice light, his movements gentle. She didn't need to know the strength of his rage.

"Had to protect her, Daddy." Harper sniffled.

"Yeah, but your mother has had her for a while now, huh?" He had to remain calm. "Your mom won't let anything happen to her. You know she's always wanted a hedgehog in the pride."

He wasn't lying. It'd been a joke for years. But that wasn't why his mate would protect the little bit of nothing in the bathroom. He'd taken one look at that ball of slobber-covered quills and one glance at Maya's eyes, and he knew the hedgehog was here to stay—even if she hadn't acknowledged the choice at the time.

"We have to keep her safe, Dad. You and Uncle Brute and Uncle Grayson and Uncle Neal..." Harper rushed through the names of her mother's guards and some of the other strongest males in the pride. "And East and West, Dad."

East he could understand. Weston though... "Baby, you know how West can be..."

"He won't hurt her." Harper shook her head. "He won't. He just..." She shrugged.

Yeah, Weston *just*...

"Doesn't she have parents? Or a pack?" He still didn't understand why groups of hedgehogs called themselves a pack, but he wasn't gonna ask. "I bet someone's missing her, huh?"

Harper just shook her head, another one of those heartbreaking tears escaping before she rubbed her nose on Alex's chest. Another blob of snot on his shirt. Nice. He'd gotten used to never having clean clothes, but he'd been hoping that since Harper was getting older... Yeah, he mentally sighed. Wasn't happening.

"He killed her mommy." Harper squished her face onto his chest and whispered against his shirt. "I saw, Dad. I smelled a human, and so I went to see."

They'd talk about her chasing after humans as a shifted lioness later.

"I followed the trail like you taught me." If only he hadn't taught her so well. "And I found them arguing by the clearing."

Fuck but she'd gone far, and they'd have a *serious* talk about that later. As Maya often called them, it was time for a Come to Jesus Meeting. "What were they arguing about, sweetheart?"

"The mommy had a baby, but it wasn't the tiger's baby. It was supposed to be, but the Gaian Moon came. The baby took a long time to shift and she just did, and it was a hedgehog, not a tiger." Alex and Maya hadn't had the *full* talk about the Gaian Moon and the role it played in ensuring the continuance of their kind, but Harper had a broad picture understanding.

"Uh-huh." He quietly encouraged her to continue.

"He said he was gonna kill the mommy and the baby." She pulled away from him then, blue eyes so like her mother's filled with pain and a desperate need to be believed. "I couldn't let him, Dad. I couldn't." She shook her head, leave-strewn strands whipping back and forth. "I had to stop him."

"You did good, sweetheart. We always help..."

"Those who can't help themselves. Except Aunt Carly and Aunt Elly because they're prey that can bite." Harper grinned and snapped her teeth together, a glimmer of her true self peeking out.

"Exactly. So what did you do?"

"I sniffed for a different kind of shifter. The man smelled like Finn on two legs and she was human, and I know what pride smells like."

Damn he was proud of her. Smart as hell and even stronger. It scared the shit out of him. But she knew a tiger's scent from

Finn—a transplant from the UK—and pride, no matter the species, shared a little something in their scents.

"He killed her while I was looking, and then I found the hedgehog and snatched her and came home." Harper's lower lip trembled. "But he heard me. I wasn't quiet enough and you had to—"

"Protect the pride and my family. Like I always do and always will, huh?"

Harper nodded and sniffled, running her forearm across her nose. Better her own arm than his shirt again.

"Knock, knock," Maya's soft voice drifted to him through Harper's open door and they both turned their attention to her.

To her and the blanket wrapped girl she held.

"Mommy?" Hope and heartache filled Harper's tone and he rubbed his daughter's back, comforting her.

"Hey, guys, *this*," Maya tugged on an edge of the blanket, revealing a mass of tangled dark hair. "Is Lark."

One blue eye flicked to him and then Lark snapped it closed once more, small hands clinging even more tightly to Maya.

"Lark?" Harper sat up straight, that inquisitive, sharp mind going to work. "She's a hedgehog."

"Named Lark." Maya's lips twitched.

"A lark is a bird, *mom*."

"Lark is also a hedgehog, *Dazs*."

"Mom." Harper narrowed her eyes. "I'm not wrong. You only get to call me Dazs when I'm wrong or in trouble, and I didn't do anything wrong. Daddy said so."

That earned him a raised eyebrow from his mate and he just shrugged. "He deserved what he got."

Especially after what he'd done to the mother. Harper hadn't

41

given any details—yet—but he imagined she'd have a round of nightmares for a while. Tigers sometimes played with their food.

"Uh-huh." Lark whined and Maya snapped into *mom* mode in an instant, gently rocking the girl while whispering a soft *shhh* to her. "Lark's last name is Hawkins. Like her mother's. She even smells a little bit like her *human* mommy."

Alex frowned, mind flipping through the hedgehog families he knew. There was a bar between Ridgeville and Stratton—Honey's—and the owner's mate was the alpha of the local hedgehog pack. "Blake doesn't have any Hawkins'. She's not married to a local." He flicked his attention to Harper and then back to his mate. "And from what I understand, the tiger wasn't... And I don't know of any with that name either or recognize him."

And fuck he knew just about everyone. They both did. Between shifters going through Ridgeville and the time they spent keeping shifters safe from Freedom and HSE, they met a lot of shifters of *every* species.

"Think bigger picture, non-furry Hawkins." Maya opened her eyes wide and gave him a serious look. One that said he needed to remember something. Well, what the fuck was he supposed to remember?

He stared at Maya.

Maya stared at him.

He still stared at Maya.

"Oh fuck no." Alex shook his head. "You're fucking joking."

"Daddy." Harper poked him. "Daddy..."

"One second, sweetheart." He wrapped his hand around her tiny fist. "Daddy's having a panic attack."

"Dad, Primes don't panic." Harper tugged against his hold, but he wasn't ready to let her go just yet.

He also wasn't done panicking—whether they did or not. Hard not to when staring at the small child in his mate's arms as if it was the devil incarnate. "And she's related to…"

"Her grandfather."

Shit, fuck, damn, and growl. She was the devil's spawn once removed then.

That didn't change the fact that she was innocent. Innocent and in need of protection, which Ridgeville would give her. Not just because Alex demanded it as the Prime, but because the pride knew what the HSE was capable of. And Lark's grandfather—her whole family—*was* the HSE. The anti-shifter organization was built from the ground up by the Hawkins family.

Except, apparently, Lark's mother, who'd fucked a shifter and given birth to a werehedgehog daughter. But who the hell was her father?

# CHAPTER FIVE

Being a total badass means *because I said so* applies to every part of your life. It also means having a mate who can back up that *I said so* part of your world." – Maya O'Connell, Prima of the Ridgeville pride and woman whose *I said so* is handled by Alex.

They strode into the living room side by side, secure in the knowledge that the twins were holed up in Easton's room while Harper and little Lark were curled together in Harper's bed. They slept the sleep of innocent children who didn't have a care in the world while some of the older cubs, pups, and kits crowded the floor. The moment they'd been allowed in the room, the raucous menagerie of children overran the space.

Her ovaries had busted out some egg-making-shaking that made her want just *one* more kidlet. Maybe. That was when her uterus busted out with its version of *I Will Always Love You*. Except it told Maya it would always love carrying her babies.

No. *No.* She'd made her contribution to society in the form of at least one normal-ish child—Harper. Then again, Harper was an awful lot like her, and Alex always said she was...

Everyone tensed when they walked through the entry, over a dozen eyes intent on them. Half were filled with fury and the other half filled with a bloodlust she could understand. The Ovulators were a pretty bloodthirsty bunch.

She had no doubt they'd heard every word of Alex's conversation with Harper and then the one she'd shared with her mate. They knew, and now it was time to plan.

Alex went to his normal seat, the plush chair comfortable and worn-in after all these years. The second he thumped down, he tugged on her arm, pulling her into his lap. Maya didn't resist a bit when he pulled, her lioness needing his closeness after everything they'd endured. She laid her head on his shoulder, taking comfort in his touch and scent.

The Ovulators did the same, the female halves of every couple touching their mates in some way. She wasn't sure where the idea that wolves were the only tactile shifter species came from, but it was dead wrong.

Fur, feathers, or scales, touch was important.

Maya breathed deeply, letting Alex's scent soothe some of her ragged nerves, and then she pulled away, giving the room her attention.

But Alex spoke first, questioning their pride. "Ricker? Elise? News?"

Ricker shook his head. "The guys have nothing."

The *guys*—a dark as hell shifter group that was legal... and yet not. But then again, that assumed the *guys* even existed. And it wasn't as if Maya hadn't asked. Of course, Ricker had just looked at her and given her that whole "if I told you I'd have to kill you" line.

Thing was, she didn't think he was joking.

"I called Gavin." Elise drew everyone's attention, and Brute tightened his hold on his little fox mate. Elise's brother, Gavin, was the master of all things electronic with the council and also mated to a lioness from Ridgeville. "He said there's not even a record of Lark's birth in any database. Council surveillance has remained constant on the mother—on the whole family—but if that's the daughter of Victoria Hawkins, they have no idea where she came from. They don't even know when Victoria would have come into contact with shifters." Elise shook her head. "HSE takes *prisoners*," she spat the word. "But Victoria has never been to an HSE compound or had an opportunity to come into contact with them."

"Maybe she met someone the council sent in undercover?" Maya raised her eyebrows. "Someone the council..." she swallowed hard, not liking what could have happened to a fellow shifter, "lost?"

The fox shook her head again. "According to Gavin, the council has pulled out of ops and cut back to distance surveillance only."

Alex's growl vibrated through her body and Maya added her own to the mix. It wasn't just shock that had her lioness reacting to the news, but bone-deep rage as well. Soon Brute and Harding joined in—Deuce, Wyatt, and Neal adding their own. The Ovulators wouldn't be left out, either—each woman hating the council's actions.

"Since when?" Alex snarled and a jolt rippled over his body. Fur tickled her skin and the hand clutching her thigh tightened, nails pricking her skin.

Maya had reasons for her rage—for her hatred at what HSE had done to so many—but Alex's fury reached farther back, into the past when he'd lost friends to the organization.

The council had promised to keep tabs on every anti-shifter organization going forward. Every movement, every communication. If a leader sneezed, they'd know about it.

Elise shook her head. "I don't know. Gavin doesn't either. He found several conflicting reports but he didn't go too deep. He will if we want him to, but that kind of data mining needs to be planned. Not spur of the moment."

Which Maya understood. Hated, but understood.

Had she mentioned hated?

Like any government organization—shifter or not—hacking was a tiny bit frowned upon. Digging through council records without authorization? Yeah, that could end... badly. Painfully.

Deadly?

She hoped not. Like, seriously.

"So where does that leave us?" Grayson spoke up, his amber eyes focused on Alex, not Maya. He was the second and reported to Alex. It made sense that he'd look to his Prime for guidance.

Maya's guards knew better and looked to her. They'd chased her across state lines—more than once—after some truly awesomesauce ideas. They also knew of her penchant for rescuing whether rescue was needed or not.

In her mind, the whole rescue thing was just a matter of opinion, and if anyone had an opinion that didn't match hers, she'd take a pin to their onion.

Which... didn't really make sense in the traditional way, but it confused others just enough that she got her way before they could say no.

Score!

As for where it left them...

Right. The guards were looking to her for the answer. "We now have a new member of the Ridgeville pride. Her name is Lark O'Connell and she's a distant relative of Alex's. Her parents were tragically killed in a hunting accident—"

"At least one of her parents is a hedgehog," Alex drawled, and she glared at her mate.

"What? Hedgehogs can't be hunted in the wild? They exist only in pet shops and little kids' bedrooms?" Because really, they had to be wild at some point. Something couldn't become domesticated if it was never undomesticated. Whatever. Maya harrumphed and deepened her glare. "As I was *say-ing…*" She turned her attention to the group. "Lark O'Connell is an orphaned cousin. Elise?" The fox raised her eyebrows in question, but remained silent. "Can you have Gavin work that kind of magic? He can't dig, but he can finagle here and there, can't he? Do a little massaging?"

At least, she hoped he could.

"If he can't, he'll know someone who can." Elise grimaced. "Digging for secrets isn't something many are willing to do, but saving a little girl…" She shrugged. "It'll be done."

"Blake might have something to say about you commandeering a hedgehog shifter." Maya ignored Alex and just elbowed him in the stomach. Blake could say all he wanted. She'd just eat him the next time he shifted. No more Hedgehog Alpha, no more problems. He ignored her ignoring him and asked another question. "And the tiger?"

Maya would have added "that was killed in the most awesome display of manly manliness ever" to the question but stopped herself.

"Gone." Ricker didn't say much more but there wasn't more to say really. He'd been alive. Now he wasn't.

"What did Gavin have to say? Any trouble from that corner?"

More head shaking. More revealed about the day's events. The male who'd tried to kill Harper—had killed Lark's mother—was a loner like most tigers. They didn't form strong family attachments beyond their own mates and young. A drifter with no ties and no one to miss him now that he was gone.

And that... hurt her heart a little bit. That a shifter could be killed—justified or not—and not be missed made her gut tighten.

"Are we thinking we brush this under the rug and not say anything?" Neal spoke up, drawing the group's attention.

Maya nodded.

Alex shook his head.

Good thing she got two votes—one because she was his mate and one because she was the Queen of Booblandia and All Things Pink Bits Related.

FYI, not something that looks great on a coffee mug.

Also not something she wanted to explain to an inquisitive child when they learned to read, and her kids had learned young, dammit.

"No one has to know." She poked Alex when he continued to shake his head.

"They don't have to know about *Lark*," he pointed out. "But we're not going to have a dead tiger and not make a report. As far as the council and everyone else will be concerned, he entered our territory without permission or an invitation, killed a human, and when discovered, he attempted to kill Harper. Those are the facts. They don't change with or without Lark's presence. The closer we stay to the truth, the less chance of Lark being discovered. If her grandfather is..."

"Fine," she grumbled. She hated when he was right. Dammit. It was best to keep Lark's identity—existence—secret. If the Hawkins family had known about Lark's shifter tendencies, she wouldn't have made it past day one.

Alex just grunted at Maya. "Grayson, give Sheriff Corman a heads up and pass the word around the pride that the hedgehog isn't to be mentioned—for her own safety."

That single word would be enough to secure everyone's silence. Safety. They all wanted that for themselves and their children.

"Done." Grayson nodded, and the discussion moved on. There was no doubt Grayson would do what was needed to keep the pride—everyone—safe. He was a lot like Alex in that way.

Not as hot though.

"Good. Then we're done for tonight. Keep your guard up. Let me know if anyone sees anything out of place. If someone who's not a resident comes to town, I want to know. Period."

Alex could put the fear of God into anyone, but Maya... Well, she wanted to give them something else to fear. The most fearsome, hated thing of all... celibacy.

"If this gets fucked up, if my new little girl gets a boo-boo or is chased by a caterpillar, no one is getting nookie." She glared at each male and mentally smiled when the Ovulators all nodded along with her. Bitches had her back. "No one knows what she's been through, her past, or the identity of her shifter family. So from this second forward, she's an O'Connell. She's the daughter of the Prime and the youngest child of the Mistress of Menstruation, Baroness of Boobs, Duchess of Badonk-a-donk, Princess of Pink Bits, Queen of Quim." Maya lifted a hand and slowly made a fist, fingers curling in one-by-one. The cat leapt forward at her call, lion's nails replacing humans the very second she opened her hand. "And ho that will straight up kill a bitch for making one of her babies cry."

# CHAPTER SIX

Always fuck like no one's watching. Mainly because at any moment, the kids could walk in and you need to finish quickly." – Maya O'Connell, Prima of the Ridgeville pride and woman who loves her kids, her new hedgehog, and fucking her mate.

They were gone, the house was quiet—truly quiet—which meant Maya finally had a moment to just *be* with her mate. The dust from the last car heading down the drive still lingered in the air, the tail lights now out of sight. The darkness encroached on the yard, the black battled by the lights from inside the home.

Alex sat on the top step of the front porch and Maya plopped beside him, resting hip-to-hip with her mate—the male who hadn't threatened to kill her.

Yet.

It wasn't as if she didn't try his patience every day. At least twice that day alone.

She leaned into Alex and nuzzled his shoulder, breathing

deeply. Smoke. Dark. Hot. A tinge of sweetness.

*Mine.*

Hers just like the children inside. All hers.

Warm lips brushed her forehead, a soft precursor to a gentle nuzzle from her mate. "Tired?"

"Depends," she murmured.

Alex just chuckled. Fifteen years and he knew her too well. She was too tired for many things, but if he had sex on the brain...

"Too tired to finish what you started earlier?"

Maya tipped her head back, excitement thrumming in her veins, the desire she'd stomped on so many hours ago now flaring back to life. "Never."

"Good. C'mon."

Oh, she wanted to come all right.

Alex released her and pushed to his feet, grabbing her hand and tugging her up behind him. Except, instead of throwing her over his shoulder and carrying her inside for one night of awesome boot knocking...

He led her down the stairs, around the side of the house, and past the rose bushes she'd never quite managed to grow. Weston puked on them after eating something Easton "caught" and the ground had been barren ever since.

Maya thought "caught" was more like "found rotting in the woods."

But no one died so it was fine.

"Alex? We could..." He could just bend her over against the tree off to their right and that'd be fine.

Alex grunted. Yeah, that was a no.

"But, Alex..." She even whined. *Whined.* Like a cat in heat. Well, cats in heat yowled, but the kids were sleeping. "We..."

They rounded the last corner and—

"*Alex*," she whispered, voice suddenly lost. All day she'd yelled and growled and snarled and now…

Her mate tugged, the pressure constant while he drew her forward and beneath his arm. Those familiar lips caressed her temple, his mouth curved in one of those smug smiles she hated. He deserved to be all smug, but that didn't mean she had to like it.

"Happy anniversary." His deep tenor vibrated through her, two words that touched her heart, but what she saw touched her soul.

A near full moon.

A pristine and perfectly set table for two.

What she knew would be chilled raw beef in a nearby cooler.

And a cherry on top for dessert. In the form of a cherry wood desk. Exactly like the one they'd first fucked on all those years ago in Alex's office at Genesis.

"You didn't forget," she breathed out the words with a nearly silent whisper. She'd tried to plan her own anniversary celebration that the kids sorta destroyed. Er, ate. Then Carly decided to try, but then Alex sorta… killed a tiger. And now…

"Never, baby." He squeezed her hip and pulled, encouraging her to turn in his grip. "Forget the first day I saw you?" His eyes caressed her like a physical touch. "Scented you?" He leaned down and ran his nose along her neck, breathing deeply. He exhaled slowly, his warm, damp breath fanning over her skin. Deft fingers tugged at her top, nudging one strap of her tank top aside. "Tasted you?" He lapped at her mating mark, the deep scarring that'd stay with her forever. "Mated you?"

Alex caressed her back, palm skimming her spine, and his heat sank into her body, warming her from outside in. He didn't stop until his fingertips teased the upper curve of her ass and she wanted him to keep on going.

Maya whimpered. "But it's not until next week."

"And you planned on celebrating today," he murmured, teeth scraping her scar. "But things went a little sideways."

"But how…" Fuck it. She wasn't sure she *wanted* to know how he knew. She wanted him to just not stop.

Except he did stop. Asshole.

He stopped and pulled away and stared at her with those amber eyes that…

"I know you, Maya. I know what the little wrinkle above your left eye means." He brushed his thumb over the spot in question, though she'd never admit to having any type of wrinkles. "I know what you're thinking when your eyes have a little hint of gray." He ran a finger down her cheek. "And that you're up to something when this tiny dimple comes out to play."

"I don't know what you're talking about." Because she still refused to acknowledge anything that could be construed as a wrinkle.

"You know I love you and that I'll do any-fucking-thing to make you happy."

Maya swallowed and nodded. Yes, she did know. He'd proved it more than once in their years together. And those were just the times he knew about. There were plenty of instances—and awesomesauce adventures—that began with "I could always ask Alex…" and ended with "don't tell Alex."

"We've been through heaven and hell, Maya." His lips quirked in a rueful grin. "Sometimes in the same day. But no matter what's going on around us, I will always know what my mate is thinking. I will always do everything in my power to make her happy."

CELIA KYLE

*Alex*, she mouthed his name, unable to speak.

"I love you." He brushed the hair from her face, fingers gliding over her skin as he tucked it behind her ear. She turned her head slightly and kissed his palm, lapping at his bare skin and savoring the hints of his flavors that glided over her tongue. "I've loved you for fifteen years, through three kids and one thousand, two-hundred fifty-three threats to my cock. Gonna love you for fifteen more." His amber eyes darkened, deepening to sensuous honey. "Gonna love you for a *thousand* more."

"Even when I…" she flicked her attention to a darkened window that looked out over the back yard.

That rueful grin came back. "Complicate the hell out of my life and claim an orphan hedgehog as your daughter?"

His gaze drifted over her features, and just like he knew her every expression, she knew his. Knew that he wasn't really mad unless he had one pinched line between his eyebrows. That even when he frowned, it wasn't a true frown unless it reached his eyes.

"This is it. *We're* it. We're marking fifteen years with a slightly bigger family, but it's perfect."

"Fucking perfect." Her lips tipped up in a small grin and she pretended her eyes weren't filled with tears.

"*Freaking* perfect." He lowered his head, his lips capturing hers in a soft, gentle kiss that she felt all the way to her toes. He lapped at the seam of her mouth, making love to her lips before he gave her one last kiss and pulled away. "We have new little ears, baby. It's back to *freaking*."

Yeah, yeah it was. "It's freaking *purrfect*."

"Corny." He snorted.

"But you love me anyway?"

"Always."

"Even when I bring home hedgehogs?"

Alex rolled his eyes. "Your daughter brought home the hedgehog."

"Why is she my daughter when she brings home hedgehogs and yours when she drags a bloody carcass home?" She quirked a single brow. Because that'd happened-ish more than once.

"Maya?"

"Huh?"

"Happy anniversary." Then he was kissing her and then he was doing *more*. And Maya decided their life was pretty *fucking* perfect.

Even with a dead tiger and an orphaned hedgehog whose mother was part of the family who founded the HSE.

Even then.

### The End

# ABOUT THE AUTHOR

Ex-dance teacher, former accountant and erstwhile collectible doll salesperson, New York Times and USA Today bestselling author Celia Kyle now writes urban fantasy, science fiction (as Erin Tate), and paranormal romances for readers who:

1) Like super hunky heroes (they generally get furry)

2) Totally dig beautiful women (who have a few more curves than the average lady)

3) Love laughing in (and out of) bed.

It goes without saying that there's always a happily-ever-after for her characters, even if there are a few road bumps along the way.

Today she lives in Central Florida and writes full-time with the support of her loving husband and two finicky cats. (Who hate each other with a passion unrivaled. What's up with that?)

Find Celia on the web…
www.celiakyle.com
celia@celiakyle.me

CPSIA information can be obtained
at www.ICGtesting.com
Printed in the USA
LVHW04s2309131018
593517LV00001B/180/P

9 781548 279769